The D

By Ronald Baldwin

Chapter one.

Once upon a time, in a land far beyond the reach of human maps, there lay a mystical forest known as Eldergrove. In the heart of this enchanted woodland, nestled among ancient trees and shimmering lakes, lived a mighty dragon named Eldorath. Eldorath was not like other dragons; his scales shimmered like precious gems, and his eyes held the wisdom of a thousand years. Despite his fearsome appearance, Eldorath was known throughout the land as a gentle and wise creature, revered by all who knew him. One day, as the sun dipped below the horizon, casting a golden glow over Eldergrove, a young maiden named Aria ventured into the forest. Aria was a healer from a nearby village, renowned for her kindness and her ability to cure even the gravest of ailments. Yet, despite her gifts, she was deeply troubled. Her village was suffering from a terrible drought, and no amount of her healing could bring back the much-needed rain. Desperate and driven by tales of Eldorath's wisdom, Aria set out to find the dragon. She walked for days, guided by the whispers of the forest, until she reached a shimmering lake that reflected the twilight sky. There, on the shore, she found Eldorath, his massive form curled around a cluster of ancient stones. "Great

Eldorath," Aria called out, her voice trembling with both awe and fear. "I come seeking your wisdom. My village suffers from a drought, and our crops wither. Without rain, we will surely perish." Eldorath lifted his head, his eyes glowing softly in the dim light. "Child, I feel your sorrow," he rumbled. "The balance of nature has been disrupted, and it is a matter beyond simple magic or medicine." Aria's heart sank, but she refused to give up. "Please, there must be something I can do. Is there no way to restore the rain?" The dragon considered her words carefully before speaking again. "There is a way, but it requires great sacrifice and courage. Deep within this forest lies a hidden spring, guarded by ancient magic. The spring holds the power to bring rain, but to awaken it, one must offer the purest of tears—tears shed not for oneself, but for others." Aria's eyes widened. "But how can I find such tears?" "You already possess them," Eldorath replied, a gentle smile touching his fearsome face. "You must think of your village, of the lives that depend on you. When your heart is true, the tears will come." With renewed determination, Aria thanked Eldorath and set out to find the hidden spring. She journeyed through the dense forest, facing trials and challenges that tested her resolve. Finally, after what felt like an eternity, she stumbled upon the spring, its waters glistening like liquid silver. Kneeling beside it, Aria closed her eyes and thought of her village—the children playing in the fields, the elders sharing stories by the fire, the hope and life that once filled every corner. Tears welled up in her eyes, not from despair, but from love and compassion. As the first tear fell into the spring, the water began to glow, and a gentle rain started to fall. The rain grew stronger, soaking the parched earth, and Aria knew her village was saved. She made her way back, exhausted but triumphant, only to find Eldorath waiting for her at the forest's edge. "You have done well, Aria," the dragon said softly. "Your tears were pure, and your heart true. Your village will flourish once more." With a grateful heart, Aria bowed to Eldorath. "Thank you, great dragon. I will never forget your kindness." And so, the village was saved, and the legend of Eldorath and the dragon's tears spread far and wide, a testament to the power of selflessness and love. Aria continued her work as a healer, always carrying the memory of her journey and the dragon who taught her that the greatest magic of all comes from a heart willing to sacrifice for others.

chapter.2

Years passed, and Aria's village thrived under the bountiful rains and abundant harvests. Eldorath, ever watchful, continued to guard Eldergrove, his presence a silent protector over the land he cherished. The legend of the dragon's tears became a story told to children, a symbol of hope and selflessness. Aria, now older and wiser, had become the village elder. She was beloved by all, her kindness and wisdom guiding the village through every challenge. One day, a young boy named Lukas approached her with worry etched on his face. "Elder Aria," he began, his voice trembling, "my sister has fallen gravely ill, and no remedy I try seems to help her. I've heard the stories about your journey to the dragon. Can you help her as you once helped our village?" Aria looked into Lukas's eyes and saw the same desperation she had once felt. "Take me to her," she said, gathering her herbs and potions. They made their way to Lukas's home, where his sister, Lila, lay pale and weak. Aria tried every remedy she knew, but Lila's condition did not improve. Sitting by Lila's bedside, Aria realized the illness was not ordinary; it seemed to be caused by a curse. She needed Eldorath's wisdom once more. That evening, under the cover of twilight, Aria set off for Eldergrove. The journey was familiar, yet each step felt heavier with the weight of years and worry. Reaching the shimmering lake, she called out to Eldorath. "Great Eldorath, I seek your wisdom once again. A young girl in my village is gravely ill, and no remedy can cure her. I fear it is a curse." Eldorath emerged from the shadows, his eyes filled with recognition and concern. "Aria, my old friend, it is good to see you. The curse you speak of is dark magic, and it is not easily undone." "Is there a way to save her?" Aria pleaded, her voice filled with hope and fear. "There is," Eldorath replied. "The curse can be broken by the tears of the one who cast it. However, finding the caster and obtaining their tears will not be easy." Aria's determination did not waver. "Tell me what I must do." Eldorath nodded. "You must journey to the Dark Mountains, where the sorcerer who cast the curse resides. Confront him and obtain his tears, but be cautious. His heart is filled with malice." Aria thanked Eldorath and set off on her journey. The path to the Dark Mountains was treacherous, filled with perilous cliffs and shadowy

4

creatures. But Aria pressed on, her heart steadfast with the memory of the lives she had saved before. At the peak of the mountains, she found the sorcerer's lair, a dark and foreboding castle. Entering cautiously, she confronted the sorcerer, a gaunt figure cloaked in shadows. "Why have you come here, old woman?" the sorcerer hissed. "I have come to save a child you have cursed," Aria replied, her voice steady. "I need your tears to break the curse." The sorcerer laughed, a cruel and bitter sound. "You think you can demand anything of me?" Aria stood her ground, her gaze unwavering. "I ask not for myself, but for an innocent child. Please, show mercy." For a moment, something flickered in the sorcerer's eyes—remorse, perhaps, or a long-buried memory. He turned away, and when he faced Aria again, there were tears in his eyes. "Long ago, I was a kind man, but betrayal turned my heart to stone. I cannot undo my past, but if my tears can save an innocent, then take them." The sorcerer wept, his tears falling into a vial Aria held out. With the tears in hand, she hurried back to the village, her heart racing against time. Back at Lukas's home, Aria carefully administered the sorcerer's tears to Lila. As the first tear touched her lips, a soft glow enveloped her, and her eyes fluttered open. The curse was broken. The village rejoiced, and Lukas hugged Aria tightly. "Thank you, Elder Aria. You've saved my sister." Aria smiled, her heart full. "It was not I alone who saved her, but the compassion and change within the sorcerer." News of the sorcerer's redemption and Lila's recovery spread, and the legend of Eldorath and Aria grew, inspiring generations to come. In the heart of Eldergrove, Eldorath watched over his realm, knowing that true magic lay not in power, but in the purity of one's heart.

Chapter.3

Years turned into decades, and the story of Aria's bravery, the sorcerer's redemption, and Eldorath's wisdom became woven into the very fabric of the village's history. Eldergrove remained a place of wonder and mystery, its guardian dragon a symbol of hope and protection. Aria, now a venerable elder, continued to guide her people with kindness and wisdom. But as time passed, a new shadow loomed over the land. A creeping blight began to spread from the edges of Eldergrove, poisoning the soil and withering the plants. The villagers were terrified, and even Aria's extensive knowledge of herbs and remedies could not halt the blight's advance. One evening, as the sun set in a blood-red sky, Aria gathered the village council. "This blight is unlike anything we have faced before," she said gravely. "It threatens not only our village but all of Eldergrove. We must seek Eldorath's guidance once more." The villagers, their faces lined with worry, agreed. A young woman named Elara, who had grown up hearing tales of Aria's adventures, stepped forward. "Elder Aria, let me accompany you. I wish to learn from you and aid our village in any way I can." Aria saw the determination in Elara's eyes and nodded. "Very well, Elara. We will face this challenge together." The journey to Eldergrove was arduous, but

Aria and Elara pressed on, driven by their love for their home. As they reached the shimmering lake, Eldorath appeared, his majestic form casting a shadow over the water. "Aria, it is good to see you," Eldorath rumbled, his voice filled with warmth. "And who is this young one?" "This is Elara," Aria introduced her. "She is brave and wishes to help save our village from a terrible blight." Eldorath's eyes softened as he looked at Elara. "Welcome, Elara. You have a courageous heart. The blight you speak of is a manifestation of dark magic, born from deep within the earth. To cleanse it, you must retrieve the Tears of the Earth, a powerful essence hidden in the depths of the ancient caves beneath Eldergrove." Aria and Elara listened intently as Eldorath continued. "The caves are treacherous, filled with traps and creatures that guard the Tears. Only those with pure intentions can succeed." Aria thanked Eldorath, and together with Elara, set off toward the ancient caves. The entrance was hidden beneath a tangle of roots and vines, and as they ventured inside, the air grew cool and damp. The cave walls glittered with crystals, casting an eerie glow. They encountered numerous challenges— narrow passages, sudden drops, and creatures that lurked in the shadows. But with Aria's wisdom and Elara's agility, they navigated each obstacle, their bond growing stronger with every step. Finally, they reached the heart of the cave, where a crystal pool shimmered with a radiant light. Suspended above it were the Tears of the Earth, droplets of pure essence that glowed with an ethereal beauty. Aria approached the pool, her hands trembling with reverence. "Elara, we must be careful. The magic here is ancient and powerful." Elara nodded, her eyes wide with wonder. Together, they gently collected the Tears, feeling their warmth and energy fill them with hope. As they made their way back to the surface, the cave seemed to shift around them, as if acknowledging their success. When they emerged into the sunlight, Eldorath was waiting for them. "You have done well," the dragon said, his voice filled with pride. "With the Tears of the Earth, you can cleanse the blight and restore balance to Eldergrove." Back in the village, Aria and Elara carefully distributed the Tears, their pure essence seeping into the soil and cleansing it of the dark magic. Slowly, the blight receded, and life returned to the land. The villagers rejoiced, their hearts filled with gratitude and hope. Elara, now a hero in her own right, stood beside Aria, who smiled with pride. "You have shown great courage and wisdom, Elara. The future of our village is bright with leaders like you." The legend of the Tears of the Earth and the bravery of Aria and Elara became a new chapter in the village's history, a testament to the enduring power of courage, wisdom, and selflessness. Eldergrove flourished once more, and Eldorath, the ever-watchful guardian, knew that the spirit of the land would remain strong for generations to come.

Chapter.4

Years passed, and Elara became a respected leader in the village, much like Aria before her. Eldergrove flourished, its beauty and vitality a testament to the bravery and wisdom of those who had protected it. The village enjoyed peace and prosperity, and the stories of Aria, Elara, and Eldorath became cherished legends. However, peace in such a magical land is always tenuous. One fateful day, a stranger arrived at the village gates. His name was Kael, a weary traveler with dark eyes that hinted at a troubled past. He carried with him an old, tattered map and tales of an ancient relic known as the Heart of Eldergrove—a gem said to possess the power to control the very essence of the forest. Elara, now the village elder, greeted Kael with cautious curiosity. "What brings you to our village, traveler?" Kael bowed respectfully. "Elder Elara, I have journeyed far in search of the Heart of Eldergrove. It is said to be hidden deep within this forest, and its power could protect your village from any future threats." Elara's eyes narrowed. "The Heart of Eldergrove is a legend. Even if it exists, such power can be dangerous in the wrong hands." Kael nodded. "I understand your caution, but I assure you, my intentions are pure. I wish only to help." Despite her reservations, Elara decided to consult Eldorath. Together with Kael, she ventured once more into Eldergrove, where the ancient dragon awaited. "Eldorath," Elara called out as they approached the shimmering lake. "We seek your guidance about the Heart of Eldergrove." Eldorath emerged from the shadows, his eyes gleaming with ancient wisdom. "The Heart of Eldergrove is real, but it is not what many believe. It is not a gem, but a sacred tree, the very heart of the forest itself. Its roots run deep, connecting all life within Eldergrove. To seek it is to seek the very soul of the forest." Kael listened intently. "Great Eldorath, if we find the Heart, can we use its power to ensure the forest's protection forever?" Eldorath's gaze shifted to Kael, scrutinizing the traveler. "The Heart can indeed protect, but it must never be exploited for personal gain. It is a guardian's responsibility, not a weapon." Elara turned to Kael. "We will seek the Heart together, but you must understand the gravity of this task." Kael nodded solemnly. "I understand, Elder Elara. I am committed to protecting this land." The journey to the Heart of Eldergrove was unlike any Elara and Kael had undertaken. The forest seemed to come alive around them, guiding their steps and testing their resolve. They faced challenges that required both strength and compassion, proving their worthiness at every turn. Finally, they reached a secluded grove, bathed in an ethereal light. At its center stood a magnificent tree, its bark shimmering with the same radiant glow as the Tears of the Earth. This was the Heart of Eldergrove. Elara and Kael approached the tree with reverence. As they drew near, the ground trembled, and the tree's roots began to move, forming an intricate pattern on the forest floor. Eldorath appeared, his presence filling the grove with a sense of profound peace. "You have found the Heart," Eldorath said. "But now you must prove your intentions. The Heart will only respond to those who seek to protect and nurture." Elara stepped forward, her voice steady. "I pledge to protect Eldergrove and its people, to ensure the balance of nature and the well-being of all who live here." Kael followed suit. "I pledge to use my knowledge and strength to guard this forest, to honor its ancient magic, and to ensure it remains a sanctuary for future generations." The tree's roots glowed brighter, and a soft, harmonious hum filled the air. The Heart of Eldergrove accepted their vows, and its power flowed through them, imbuing them with a deep connection to the forest. Eldorath smiled, a rare expression of pure joy. "You have proven yourselves true guardians of Eldergrove. The forest is safe in your hands." Elara and Kael returned to the village, their hearts filled with a profound sense of purpose. The village celebrated their return, and the story of their quest became another cherished legend. Kael decided to stay, becoming a trusted protector and advisor, his dark past giving way to a brighter future. Under the watchful eyes of Elara, Kael, and Eldorath, Eldergrove thrived as never before. The village grew, its people living in harmony with the magical forest that protected them. And so, the legend of the dragon's tears, the Heart of Eldergrove, and the brave guardians who defended it continued to inspire generations, a testament to the enduring power of courage, wisdom, and love.

Chapter. 5

Years flowed by, and the village continued to thrive under the watchful eyes of Elara, Kael, and Eldorath. The balance of nature was maintained, and peace reigned throughout Eldergrove. Yet, as the village prospered, whispers of unrest began to reach its borders. The distant Kingdom of Aerith, a land known for its greed and ambition, had caught wind of

Eldergrove's magical essence and the Heart of Eldergrove. One crisp autumn morning, a scout arrived breathless at the village gates, bringing dire news. "Elder Elara, a massive army from Aerith marches towards Eldergrove! They seek to claim the Heart for their own." Elara, though seasoned and wise, felt a chill run through her. The villagers gathered in fear, and she called an emergency council meeting with Kael and other trusted leaders. "We must protect Eldergrove at all costs," Elara declared. "This forest has given us life and prosperity. We cannot let it fall into the hands of those who would exploit it." Kael stood by her side, his eyes fierce with determination. "We will fight to defend our home. Eldorath's guidance will be crucial in this battle." As the village prepared for the impending invasion, Elara and Kael once more journeyed to the heart of Eldergrove, seeking Eldorath's counsel. The ancient dragon awaited them, his presence as commanding as ever. "Eldorath, the Kingdom of Aerith marches upon us," Elara said, her voice steady despite the gravity of the situation. "How can we protect Eldergrove and the Heart?" Eldorath's eyes burned with a fierce light. "The Heart of Eldergrove is powerful, but it is not meant to be used as a weapon. The strength of Eldergrove lies in its unity and the purity of its protectors' hearts." Kael clenched his fists. "We will fight with all we have. But how can we ensure victory against such overwhelming numbers?" Eldorath's gaze softened. "You must rally the spirits of Eldergrove. The forest is alive with ancient beings—dryads, fae, and other magical creatures. They will aid you if they see your cause is just." With renewed resolve, Elara and Kael returned to the village and began the task of rallying their people and allies. They called upon the ancient spirits of the forest, who emerged from the depths of Eldergrove, their ethereal forms shimmering with magic. The day of battle arrived, and the village stood ready. The army of Aerith, vast and imposing, approached with a thunderous roar. Yet, Elara, Kael, and the villagers held their ground, bolstered by the presence of the forest spirits. As the armies clashed, Eldergrove itself seemed to come alive. Trees moved to block enemy paths, roots entangled soldiers, and magical creatures launched attacks from the shadows. Elara fought with the wisdom and agility of her years, while Kael led with unparalleled bravery, his dark past now a distant memory. In the midst of the chaos, a figure cloaked in darkness advanced towards the Heart of Eldergrove. Elara recognized him as the sorcerer they had once redeemed. His eyes, once filled with remorse, now burned with greed. "Stay back!" Elara shouted, her voice echoing with authority. "The Heart is not for the taking!" The sorcerer sneered. "You are a fool to think you can keep such power hidden. It belongs to those strong enough to wield it." As he advanced, Kael intercepted him, their swords clashing with sparks of magic. The battle between them was fierce, but Kael's resolve, forged through years of protection and redemption, proved stronger. With a final, powerful strike, Kael disarmed the sorcerer, who fell to the ground, defeated. Seeing their leader fall, the army of Aerith faltered. The spirits of Eldergrove, sensing victory, intensified their efforts, and the enemy was driven back, retreating into the distance. As the dust settled, Elara and Kael stood before the Heart of Eldergrove, their hearts filled with gratitude and relief. The village celebrated their triumph, the unity and bravery of its people proving more powerful than any force. Eldorath appeared, his eyes glowing with pride. "You have protected Eldergrove and proven that true strength lies in unity and the purity of purpose." Elara smiled, her eyes meeting Kael's. "We could not have done it without the help of the forest and its ancient spirits. This victory belongs to all of Eldergrove." The legend of the great battle and the unity of Eldergrove became the most cherished tale, passed down through generations. Under the guardianship of Elara, Kael, and the ever-watchful Eldorath, the village thrived, its people living in harmony with the magical forest that protected them. And so, the story of the dragon's tears, the Heart of Eldergrove, and the brave guardians who defended it continued to inspire, a testament to the enduring power of courage, wisdom, and the spirit of unity.

chapter.6

Years rolled on, and Eldergrove became known far and wide as a sanctuary of magic and harmony. Elara and Kael, now venerable elders, guided their people with wisdom and strength, while the ancient dragon Eldorath watched over them all. However, peace has a way of attracting those who wish to disrupt it. One fateful night, a brilliant meteor shower lit up the sky. The villagers marveled at the celestial display, unaware that one of the meteors was no mere rock, but a vessel carrying an unexpected visitor. As the sun rose, Elara and Kael were alerted to the presence of a mysterious figure at the edge of the village. The stranger was tall and clad in peculiar armor, unlike anything they had seen before. His eyes, a strange shade of silver, gleamed with curiosity and intent. "I am Alaric," the stranger introduced himself, bowing gracefully. "I come from a distant star to seek the Heart of Eldergrove. Its power is known even in the farthest reaches of the cosmos." Elara and Kael exchanged wary glances. "The Heart of Eldergrove is sacred and not to be taken lightly," Elara said. "Why do you seek it?" Alaric's eyes softened. "My home is in peril. Our world is dying, and we need a source of pure, untapped magic to save it. I have traveled across the stars in search of hope, and Eldergrove's legend reached my ears." Kael, ever cautious, asked, "How can we be sure your intentions are pure? The Heart has drawn many with ill intent before." Alaric placed a hand over his heart. "I understand your suspicion. Allow me to prove my sincerity. Let me help protect your village as a gesture of goodwill." Elara and Kael conferred with Eldorath, who appeared in a swirl of mist. "Eldorath, this stranger claims to come from the stars, seeking the Heart to save his world," Elara explained. "What should we do?" The ancient dragon's eyes seemed to pierce through Alaric's soul. "The Heart of Eldergrove holds immense power. If his intentions are true, we must consider his plea. But first, he must prove himself worthy." Alaric nodded, resolute. "I will do whatever it takes to earn your trust." Eldorath gave a solemn nod. "Very well. Alaric, you must journey into the depths of Eldergrove and seek the Blessing of the Ancient Ones. They are the guardians of the forest's deepest magic. Only with their blessing can you approach the Heart." Accompanied by Elara and Kael, Alaric embarked on the quest. They ventured into the untouched heart of Eldergrove, a place where the forest's magic was most potent. The journey was perilous, with trials that tested their resolve, compassion, and unity. They encountered the Ancient Ones—ethereal beings who embodied the spirit of the forest. The Ancient Ones observed them silently, their presence awe-inspiring and humbling. "Why do you seek the Heart?" one of the Ancient Ones asked, their voice resonating like a symphony. Alaric stepped forward. "My world is dying. We need the Heart's magic to restore life. I pledge to use its power for good and to protect Eldergrove's sanctity." The Ancient Ones deliberated among themselves. "We will grant you our blessing if you can demonstrate your purity of heart and selflessness. You must undergo the Trial of Elements." The Trial of Elements tested their control over the fundamental forces of nature—earth, water, fire, and air. Alaric faced each challenge with determination, guided by Elara's wisdom and Kael's bravery. He showed great respect for the forest, never taking more than he needed, always giving back in kind. When the trials were completed, the Ancient Ones bestowed their blessing upon Alaric. "You have proven yourself worthy. May the Heart's magic guide you and protect your world." With the blessing, they returned to the

Heart of Eldergrove. The sacred tree welcomed them, its roots parting to reveal a glowing, pulsating core of pure magic. Alaric approached with reverence, placing his hands on the Heart. "I pledge to use this power to heal and protect, never to exploit," he vowed. The Heart of Eldergrove glowed brighter, and a stream of energy flowed into Alaric, filling him with its ancient magic. His eyes shone with gratitude. "Thank you, Eldergrove. Your gift will save my world." Eldorath watched with approval. "Remember, Alaric, the Heart's power is a responsibility. Guard it well." With Eldergrove's blessing and the Heart's magic, Alaric prepared to return to his world. The village gathered to bid him farewell, their hearts filled with hope and gratitude. "May your journey be safe," Elara said, embracing him. "And may your world find peace." Kael clasped Alaric's hand. "Remember the spirit of Eldergrove. It will guide you." As Alaric's vessel ascended into the sky, a brilliant light trailed behind, a beacon of hope for both worlds. Eldergrove continued to flourish, its legend growing ever richer with each passing generation. And so, the story of the dragon's tears, the Heart of Eldergrove, and the guardians who protected it from threats both terrestrial and cosmic continued to inspire, a testament to the enduring power of courage, wisdom, and unity across the stars. Years turned into centuries, and the village of Eldergrove evolved into a thriving hub of magical learning and wisdom. Eldergrove became a beacon of hope, attracting scholars, mages, and seekers of truth from distant lands. Elara and Kael's legacies lived on through their descendants, who continued to uphold the values of courage, wisdom, and unity. However, with fame and prosperity came new challenges. A group of rogue mages, coveting the powerful magic of Eldergrove, began to plot in the shadows. They believed that the Heart of Eldergrove could make them the most powerful sorcerers in the world. Among the villagers, there was a young mage named Lyra. Lyra was a descendant of both Elara and Kael, and she possessed an extraordinary gift for magic. Her heart was pure, and she had been trained in the ways of the forest by the ancient spirits themselves. One night, as she meditated by the Heart of Eldergrove, Lyra felt a disturbance in the forest. The rogue mages had infiltrated Eldergrove, their dark intentions cloaked by powerful enchantments. Lyra knew she had to act swiftly to protect the Heart and the village. Lyra gathered her closest friends—Finn, a skilled archer and tracker; Mira, a healer with unparalleled knowledge of herbs and potions; and Tarek, a warrior with unmatched strength and loyalty. Together, they formed a formidable team, determined to thwart the rogue mages. Under the cover of night, they tracked the rogue mages through the forest. The intruders were led by a sorcerer named Malakar, whose ambition and greed knew no bounds. He sought to bind the Heart's magic to his will, no matter the cost. As Lyra and her friends closed in on Malakar's camp, they overheard his plans. "Once we harness the power of the Heart, Eldergrove will bow to us. The world will tremble at our feet," Malakar proclaimed. Lyra's resolve hardened. "We must stop them before they reach the Heart," she whispered to her companions. They devised a plan to divide and conquer the rogue mages. Finn and Tarek would create distractions, drawing the lesser mages away, while Lyra and Mira would confront Malakar directly. The forest spirits, sensing the impending danger

Chapter.7

They devised a plan to divide and conquer the rogue mages. Finn and Tarek would create distractions, drawing the lesser mages away, while Lyra and Mira would confront Malakar directly. The forest spirits, sensing the impending danger, offered their aid, weaving enchantments to cloak Lyra and Mira as they approached Malakar's lair. Finn and Tarek's distractions worked flawlessly. The rogue mages, lured by false sounds and illusions, scattered throughout the forest. With the path to Malakar clear, Lyra and Mira moved swiftly and silently, guided by the whispers of the ancient spirits. They found Malakar in a clearing, his dark robes billowing as he chanted incantations over a crystalline device designed to harness the Heart's magic. His eyes burned with malevolent ambition, oblivious to the approaching threat. Lyra stepped forward, her voice ringing with authority. "Malakar, your plans end here. You will not desecrate the Heart of Eldergrove." Malakar turned, a sinister smile curling on his lips. "Ah, the young protector. Do you really think you can stop me? The Heart's power will be mine." Mira, standing beside Lyra, raised her hands, invoking a protective barrier around them. "You underestimate the strength of

Eldergrove and its guardians." Malakar laughed darkly and launched a barrage of dark energy at them. Lyra countered with a powerful spell, their magic clashing in a brilliant display of light and shadow. The ground trembled as their battle intensified, each determined to protect or seize the Heart's power. Lyra's connection to the forest and her ancestors fueled her strength. She called upon the spirits of Eldergrove, their energy flowing through her. With a surge of power, she unleashed a torrent of magic, breaking through Malakar's defenses. Seeing his defeat imminent, Malakar attempted to flee, but Lyra and Mira were relentless. With a final, coordinated strike, they bound Malakar in enchanted chains, his dark magic neutralized. "You will face justice for your actions," Lyra declared, her voice unwavering. The forest spirits emerged, their presence soothing the disrupted magic of the clearing. "You have done well, Lyra," they intoned. "The Heart is safe once more." As dawn broke, Finn and Tarek returned, having successfully driven away the remaining rogue mages. The village of Eldergrove rejoiced, celebrating the bravery and unity of Lyra and her friends. Eldorath appeared, his eyes filled with pride and wisdom. "You have proven that the spirit of Eldergrove remains strong. The legacy of courage, wisdom, and unity lives on through you." Lyra bowed her head in gratitude. "We are honored to protect Eldergrove, as our ancestors did before us." With the threat vanquished, peace returned to Eldergrove. The village continued to flourish, a beacon of hope and magic. Lyra, Finn, Mira, and Tarek became legends in their own right, their story adding a new chapter to the rich tapestry of Eldergrove's history. And so, the tale of the dragon's tears, the Heart of Eldergrove, and the guardians who defended it from threats both near and far continued to inspire generations, a testament to the enduring power of courage, wisdom, and unity.

Chapter.8

As the years passed, Eldergrove remained a place of peace and prosperity under the watchful eyes of its guardians. Lyra, Finn, Mira, and Tarek continued to protect the village, passing on their knowledge and skills to future generations. One day, a new threat emerged—a dark sorceress named Selena, who wielded forbidden magic and sought to claim Eldergrove for her own. Selena had learned of the Heart of Eldergrove and believed its power could make her unstoppable. Lyra, now the village elder, sensed the impending danger and called upon her companions. "We must prepare to defend Eldergrove once more," she said, her voice filled with determination. Finn, now a seasoned warrior, nodded. "We will not let Selena harm our home. We will stand together, as we always have." Mira, her healing skills honed over the years, added, "With the spirits of Eldergrove on our side, we can overcome any threat." Tarek, his strength undiminished by time, clenched his fists. "Let us show Selena the power of unity and courage." Together, they trained the villagers, preparing them for the coming battle. The forest spirits, ever watchful, lent their aid, strengthening the village's defenses and imbuing the guardians with their ancient magic. When Selena's forces arrived, Eldergrove was ready. The battle that ensued was fierce, magic clashing with steel as the guardians and villagers fought to protect their home. Selena's dark magic was powerful, but the unity and courage of Eldergrove's defenders were stronger. In the midst of the chaos, Selena made her way toward the Heart of Eldergrove, her eyes gleaming with malice. Lyra, Finn, Mira, and Tarek intercepted her, their determination unwavering. "You will not lay a hand on the Heart," Lyra declared, her voice echoing through the clearing. Selena laughed, a sound filled with scorn. "You cannot stop me. The Heart's power will be mine." The guardians unleashed their magic, the air crackling with energy as spells collided. Selena's power was formidable, but she was no match for the combined strength of Eldergrove's protectors. With a final, mighty effort, the guardians subdued Selena, her dark magic fading into the forest. As she lay defeated, Lyra approached her, her eyes filled with compassion. "Why do you seek to harm Eldergrove?" Lyra asked, her voice soft. Selena's gaze softened, a hint of regret flickering in her eyes. "I sought power... but I see now that true power lies in unity and harmony, not in darkness and greed." With Selena's defeat, peace returned to Eldergrove once more. The village celebrated its victory, and Selena, humbled by her defeat, chose to stay and learn from Eldergrove's guardians, seeking redemption for her past actions. Under the guidance of Lyra, Finn, Mira, and Tarek, Eldergrove continued to thrive, its legacy of courage, wisdom, and unity shining brighter than ever before. And so, the story of the dragon's tears, the Heart of Eldergrove, and the guardians who protected it became a beacon of hope for all who heard it, a reminder that no darkness is too great to overcome with the light of unity and courage.

Chapter.9

As the seasons passed, Eldergrove flourished under the watchful eyes of its guardians. Selena, once a dark sorceress, had found redemption among the villagers, her knowledge of magic now used to heal and protect. One day, a messenger arrived from a distant kingdom, bearing news of a new threat—a great darkness that threatened to consume the land. The darkness was said to be ancient, born from a time before time, and it sought to engulf all in its path. Lyra, now the wisest of the elders, called upon her companions. "The time has come for us to face our greatest challenge yet. The darkness threatens not just Eldergrove, but all of existence." Finn, Mira, and Tarek nodded, their faces grim but determined. "We will stand together, as we always have," Finn declared. The guardians knew that defeating the darkness would require more than just their strength. They would need to unite all the kingdoms and realms, forging an alliance strong enough to withstand the encroaching shadows. Together, they set out on a quest to rally the forces of good. They traveled far and wide, facing trials and challenges that tested their resolve. But with each obstacle overcome, their alliance grew stronger. At last, they stood before the darkness, a swirling maelstrom of shadow and despair that threatened to consume everything in its path. The guardians, joined by the armies of the allied kingdoms, prepared for the final battle. The battle was fierce, the darkness unleashing horrors beyond imagination. But the guardians fought with a courage born of unity, their hearts fueled by the knowledge that they fought not just for their homes, but for all existence. In the midst of the chaos, Selena stepped forward, her voice strong and clear. "I have seen the darkness within myself, and I have learned that true power lies in embracing the light." With those words, Selena unleashed a torrent of pure, radiant magic, pushing back the darkness and revealing a glimmer of hope. Inspired by her example, the guardians and their allies fought with renewed vigor, their unity shining like a beacon in the darkness. As the last remnants of the darkness faded, a new dawn broke over the land. The kingdoms and realms, once divided, now stood united, bound by the courage and wisdom of Eldergrove's guardians. With the darkness defeated, Lyra, Finn, Mira, Tarek, and Selena returned to Eldergrove as heroes. The village rejoiced, celebrating their bravery and unity. And as they looked out over the land, they knew that as long as the spirit of courage, wisdom, and unity lived on, no darkness could ever truly prevail. And so, the story of the dragon's tears, the Heart of Eldergrove, and the guardians who protected it became a legend for the ages, a reminder that even in the darkest of times, the light of unity and courage will always prevail.

Chapter.10

With the darkness vanquished and peace restored to the land, Eldergrove entered a new era of prosperity and harmony. The alliance forged in battle remained strong, and the kingdoms and realms worked together to rebuild and grow. Lyra, Finn, Mira, Tarek, and Selena continued to protect Eldergrove, their bonds of friendship and unity stronger than ever. Together, they ensured that the lessons learned from their trials were passed down to future generations, so that the spirit of courage, wisdom, and unity would never fade. As the years passed, Eldergrove became a symbol of hope and inspiration for all who knew its story. Travelers from far and wide came to learn from its guardians and to bask in the magic of the forest. And though the world faced new challenges and threats, the spirit of Eldergrove endured, a beacon of light in a world that sometimes seemed dark and troubled. One day, as Lyra sat by the Heart of Eldergrove, watching the sun set over the forest, she reflected on the journey that had brought her here. She thought of all the trials and challenges she had faced, and of the friends who had stood by her side through it all. "We have faced many challenges together," she said softly to the Heart. "But as long as we remain united, there is nothing we cannot overcome." The Heart pulsed with a warm, reassuring energy, a silent affirmation of her words. And as the stars began to twinkle in the evening sky, Lyra knew that no matter what the future held, as long as the spirit of courage, wisdom, and unity lived on in Eldergrove, there would always be hope for a brighter tomorrow. And so, the legend of the dragon's tears, the Heart of Eldergrove, and the guardians who protected it faded into myth and legend, but the spirit of their story lived on in the hearts of all who heard it, a reminder that no matter how dark the night, the light of unity and courage would always shine through.

Chapter.11

As time passed, Eldergrove's legend grew, becoming a story told to children around hearth fires, a tale of bravery, unity, and the enduring power of hope. The village itself became a place of pilgrimage, where those seeking wisdom and inspiration would come to walk among the ancient trees and feel the magic that lingered in the air. Lyra, Finn, Mira, Tarek, and Selena grew old, their days filled with peace and contentment. They passed their knowledge and skills on to the next generation, ensuring that the guardians of Eldergrove would always be ready to defend their home should the need arise. One day, a young girl named Elowen arrived at Eldergrove's gates. She was a dreamer, with a heart full of curiosity and a thirst for adventure. She had heard the stories of Eldergrove and its guardians and had come seeking the truth behind the legends. As Elowen wandered through the village, she felt a deep sense of peace and belonging. She knew that she had found a place where she could learn and grow, where she could become the person she was meant to be. She sought out Lyra, now the eldest of the guardians, and asked to be trained in the ways of the forest. Lyra saw something special in the young girl and agreed to take her under her wing. Under Lyra's guidance, Elowen learned the ways of the forest, honing her skills in magic, combat, and diplomacy. She studied the history of Eldergrove, uncovering ancient secrets and forgotten truths. And as she grew, so too did her connection to the Heart of Eldergrove, until she could feel its magic coursing through her veins. One day, as Elowen stood before the Heart, she felt a strange stirring in the air. She sensed that a new threat was approaching, one unlike any that Eldergrove had faced before. She sought out the other guardians, who gathered in the clearing before the Heart. Together, they gazed out into the forest, where a dark shadow was spreading, blotting out the light of the sun. "It is the darkness," Mira whispered, her voice filled with fear. "It has returned." The guardians knew that they must act quickly to protect Eldergrove and all that they held dear. They called upon the spirits of the forest, who answered with a chorus of voices that seemed to shake the very ground beneath their feet. "We must unite once more," Finn declared, his voice strong and unwavering. "For Eldergrove, for each other, for all of existence." And so, the guardians and Elowen set out to rally the kingdoms and realms once more, to forge an alliance strong enough to stand against the darkness. They knew that the road ahead would be long and difficult, but they also knew that as long as they remained united, there was nothing they could not overcome. And as they set out on their journey, the Heart of Eldergrove pulsed with a steady, reassuring beat, a beacon of hope in the encroaching darkness.

Chapter.12

The journey to rally the kingdoms and realms was long and arduous, filled with challenges and dangers at every turn. But the guardians and Elowen were undaunted, their determination unwavering as they traveled through forests, across mountains, and over seas. Along the way, they encountered allies old and new, each with their own skills and strengths to offer. Together, they formed a formidable alliance, united in their determination to stand against the darkness. As they drew closer to the source of the darkness, they could feel its malevolent presence growing stronger. The land around them withered and died, the very air thick with despair. At last, they reached the edge of the darkness, a swirling maelstrom of shadow and dread that seemed to stretch on forever. The guardians and their allies stood before it, steeling themselves for the battle ahead. "We cannot let the darkness consume us," Lyra said, her voice steady. "We must fight with all our strength, for the sake of Eldergrove and all of existence." With a cry of defiance, they charged into the darkness, their weapons and magic blazing. The battle was fierce, the darkness lashing out with tendrils of shadow that sought to overwhelm them. But the guardians and their allies fought with a courage born of unity, their hearts filled with the light of hope. They pushed back against the darkness, driving it back bit by bit. As the battle raged on, Elowen felt a surge of power within her. She reached out to the Heart of Eldergrove, calling upon its magic to aid her. The Heart responded, filling her with a radiant light that burned away the darkness around her. With a mighty cry, Elowen unleashed a wave of pure, white light that surged through the darkness, scattering it like smoke in the wind. The land around them began to heal, the withered plants springing back to life as if by magic. The darkness, weakened and in retreat, began to recede, vanishing into the shadows from whence it came. The guardians and their allies stood victorious, their unity and courage having saved Eldergrove and all of existence from certain doom. As they returned to Eldergrove, they were greeted as heroes, their names spoken in awe and reverence. The village rejoiced, celebrating their victory with feasting and song. But the guardians knew that their work was not yet done. The darkness had been defeated, but it would always linger at the edges of existence, waiting for an opportunity to return. And so, they vowed to remain vigilant, to stand ready to defend Eldergrove and all that they held dear. For as long as the spirit of courage, wisdom, and unity lived on in their hearts, they knew that they would always be able to face whatever challenges the future might bring.

Chapter.13

Years passed, and Eldergrove prospered under the watchful eyes of its guardians. Elowen had grown into a wise and powerful leader, her connection to the Heart of Eldergrove deepening with each passing day. One day, a new threat emerged—a powerful sorcerer named Drakus, who sought to harness the magic of Eldergrove for his own dark purposes. Drakus had amassed a formidable army and laid siege to the village, his dark magic sowing chaos and destruction wherever it touched. Elowen knew that they could not defeat Drakus through force alone. She called upon the spirits of the forest, who whispered to her of a way to defeat him—a way that required courage, wisdom, and unity. Elowen sought out Drakus, who stood before the Heart of Eldergrove, his eyes filled with greed and malice. "You cannot stop me, girl," he sneered. "The power of the Heart will be mine." But Elowen was undaunted. She approached Drakus, her voice calm but firm. "The Heart does not belong to you, Drakus. Its power is meant to protect and heal, not to destroy." Drakus laughed, a cruel sound that echoed through the clearing. "You are a fool, girl. The power of the Heart is mine to command." With a wave of his hand, Drakus unleashed a wave of dark energy that surged towards Elowen. But she stood her ground, raising her hands and calling upon the magic of Eldergrove. A shimmering barrier of light formed around Elowen, repelling Drakus's attack and sending him reeling. The spirits of the forest emerged, their forms radiant with magic. "You have abused the power of Eldergrove for too long, Drakus," Elowen declared. "It is time for you to leave." Drakus, realizing that he was outnumbered and outmatched, retreated, his army following close behind. The darkness that had threatened to consume Eldergrove faded, and once again, peace returned to the land. As the villagers celebrated their victory, Elowen stood before the Heart of Eldergrove, her heart full of gratitude. She knew that as long as the spirit of courage, wisdom, and unity lived on in Eldergrove, the village would always be protected. And so, the legend of the dragon's tears, the Heart of Eldergrove, and the guardians who protected it continued to inspire generations, a testament to the enduring power of hope and unity in the face of darkness.

Chapter.14

Years turned into decades, and Eldergrove remained a bastion of peace and harmony. Elowen had become a revered elder, her wisdom sought by all who came to the village seeking guidance. One day, a young boy named Alden arrived at Eldergrove's gates. He was an orphan, his parents taken by a sickness that had plagued his village. He had heard tales of Eldergrove and its guardians and had come seeking a new home, a place where he could belong. Elowen took Alden under her wing, teaching him the ways of the forest and the magic that flowed through it. She saw great potential in the young boy, a spark of courage and wisdom that reminded her of herself when she was young. As Alden grew, he became a skilled warrior and a powerful mage, his abilities rivaling even those of the legendary guardians. He was a natural leader, inspiring others with his bravery and his unwavering belief in the power of unity. One day, a new threat emerged—a mighty dragon that had awoken from its slumber deep within the mountains. The dragon, enraged by the encroachment of civilization into its territory, began to lay waste to villages and towns, its fiery breath consuming everything in its path. Elowen knew that they could not defeat the dragon through force alone. She called upon Alden and the other guardians, and together, they devised a plan to confront the dragon and convince it to leave peacefully. They journeyed to the mountains, where the dragon lay in wait, its scales gleaming in the sunlight. Alden stepped forward, his voice steady as he addressed the dragon. "Great dragon, we mean you no harm," Alden said. "We seek only peace between our peoples. Will you not hear us out?" The dragon regarded Alden with eyes that burned with ancient wisdom. "Why should I listen to you, human? You have brought nothing but destruction to my lands." Alden knew that he had to prove their sincerity. He told the dragon of Eldergrove and its guardians, of their commitment to peace and harmony, and of their belief that all beings could live together in unity. The dragon listened, and as Alden spoke, its demeanor softened. It saw in Alden a kindred spirit, a soul that longed for peace and understanding. At last, the dragon spoke. "I have seen much in my long life, but never have I encountered humans such as you. I will spare your village, and in return, I ask only for your friendship." Alden smiled, relief flooding through him. "You have our friendship, noble dragon. May it bring peace to us both." And so, the dragon returned to its lair, and peace was restored to the mountains. Alden returned to Eldergrove, hailed as a hero, his actions a testament to the enduring power of courage, wisdom, and unity. And as the villagers celebrated their victory, Elowen knew that as long as there were beings like Alden, willing to stand up for what was right, the spirit of Eldergrove would never fade.

Chapter.15

Years passed, and Alden grew into a wise and respected leader, following in Elowen's footsteps as the guardian of Eldergrove. Under his leadership, Eldergrove continued to thrive, its bonds with neighboring kingdoms and realms stronger than ever. One day, a messenger arrived at Eldergrove bearing news of a new threat—a powerful sorceress named Malora, who had risen to power and sought to conquer the land. Malora wielded dark magic unlike anything seen before, and her armies were vast and formidable. Alden knew that they could not face Malora alone. He called upon the allied kingdoms and realms, and together, they formed a great army to confront the sorceress and her forces. As the army marched towards Malora's stronghold, they encountered fierce resistance. Malora's magic was powerful, and her armies were relentless. But Alden and his allies fought with a courage born of unity, their determination unwavering. At last, they reached Malora's stronghold, a towering fortress of dark stone and twisted spires. The battle that ensued was fierce, magic and steel clashing in a cacophony of sound and light. Alden and his allies fought their way to the heart of the fortress, where they confronted Malora herself. She was a formidable opponent, her dark magic twisting and warping the very fabric of reality. But Alden was undaunted. With a cry of defiance, he unleashed his own magic, a radiant light that pierced the darkness of Malora's spells. The two forces clashed, their magic meeting in a dazzling display of power. At last,

Alden's light overwhelmed Malora's darkness, and the sorceress was defeated. As she lay defeated, her powers drained, she looked up at Alden with eyes filled with hatred and fear. "You may have won this battle, but you cannot defeat me," she spat. "I will return, and when I do, I will destroy you and everything you hold dear." But Alden was unafraid. "As long as there are beings like me, willing to stand up to tyranny and oppression, you will never succeed." With that, Malora was taken into custody, her threat neutralized. The land rejoiced, celebrating the victory of light over darkness, courage over fear, and unity over division. And as Alden stood before the Heart of Eldergrove, he knew that the spirit of courage, wisdom, and unity would always prevail, no matter what challenges the future might bring. And so, the legend of the dragon's tears, the Heart of Eldergrove, and the guardians who protected it continued to inspire generations, a testament to the enduring power of hope and unity in the face of darkness

Made in the USA
Columbia, SC
27 July 2024

39445502R00020